DIMPLE AND THE BOO

DIMPLE
AND THE BOO
THE

PIP JONES

Illustrated by
Paula Bowles

Barrington Stoke

First published in 2022 in Great Britain by
Barrington Stoke Ltd
18 Walker Street, Edinburgh, EH3 7LP

www.barringtonstoke.co.uk

A CIP catalogue record for this book is available
from the British Library upon request

ISBN: 978-1-80090-145-2

Printed by Hussar Books, Poland

This book is in a super-readable format for young readers
beginning their independent reading journey.

For my littlest niece, beautiful Evie xx

CONTENTS

CHAPTER 1
PopPop's gone

Dimple didn't want PopPop to see him cry, so he sat under the lompit tree and hid his face in his hands.

"I won't be gone long, Dimple!" PopPop told him. "Only two weeks."

"You promised we'd play hoop-ball this weekend," Dimple said sadly.

Everything had been fine until a few weeks ago, when PopPop had to close his whizzy-kart workshop.

You see, every gnome had a whizzy-kart to zoom about in, and PopPop's karts were the best.

Dimple didn't understand why
PopPop couldn't just keep his whizzy-kart
workshop at the end of the road open.
Why couldn't everything stay the same?
Why did PopPop have to go and work
somewhere else?

"I told you, Dimple," said PopPop. "Everyone wants to buy the new type of whizzy-kart now. That means I have to go and work at a new factory to make the money we need. I'm sorry it's far away.

"I'll be back before you know it," PopPop added, and he gave Dimple a big hug.

Dimple listened to PopPop's footsteps as he walked away. Then he heard PopPop's engine whizzing. He only stood up and uncovered his eyes when he couldn't hear the engine any more.

PopPop had gone. It wasn't fair.

The yard was empty apart from a single hoop-ball and the lompit tree.

Dimple's cheeks suddenly felt hot.
He kicked the lompit tree as hard as
he could.

"OUCH! GRRRRR!!" Dimple growled.

The dark green leaves shook and
something crashed down the branches.
It landed next to Dimple's foot, which was
now sore.

A lompit.

"Huh?"

The lompit looked a bit ... odd.

CHAPTER 2

The not-a-lompit

The thing at Dimple's feet was bright red and round, just like all the lompits that grew on the lompit tree.

But it wasn't shiny like a lompit. It was all fuzzy and it was ... fizzing.

With his foot, Dimple prodded the not-a-lompit.

"Wah!" Dimple jumped when he saw two shiny black eyes blinking at him.

"You're not a lompit!" Dimple said.

"**No**," said the not-a-lompit gruffly. "**I am a Boo**."

Dimple frowned. He'd never heard of a Boo before – apart from the kind of "BOO!" people shout when they want to make you jump. Dimple found that kind of Boo very annoying.

"Are you trying to make me jump, Boo?" Dimple wanted to know.

"**I am a Boo**," the Boo said again, and then it made a bubbly noise that Dimple had never heard before.

"It's supper time, Dimple!" Mama shouted from the house.

"Coming!" Dimple replied.

Quickly, without thinking, Dimple scooped up the Boo and stuffed it into his hoodie pocket before he went in.

CHAPTER 3

The plate of yucky

Mama was humming happily as she spooned the food onto two plates – but the smell in the kitchen did not make Dimple happy.

If the kitchen had smelled of fried eggs, and sweet fig pancakes for pudding, that would have cheered Dimple up a lot.

But what the kitchen smelled of was cabbage pie – and no pudding at all.

"Aw, Mama!" Dimple groaned. "Not cabbage pie again!"

"Cabbage pie is tasty and it's good for you," Mama said firmly. "Now sit down and enjoy it!"

Dimple knew right away that he was *not* going to enjoy it. PopPop's place at the table looked empty and sad.

"I miss PopPop too," Mama said as she put the plates on the table, "but he'll be back before you know it!"

Dimple huffed. He picked up his fork and shoved the cabbage pie into his mouth, then swallowed it as fast as he could.

Mama was watching him.

"Chew your food, please," she said.

Dimple frowned and began to chew, but his cheeks tingled.

His tummy suddenly felt funny, like there was something hot and red in there, fizzing and humming.

"Ewwwww! Yucky!"

"Dimple!" Mama said. "Don't be rude!"

"What? I …" Dimple didn't think he had made a sound!

He put his hand on his hot, buzzing belly, then he remembered – the Boo! It was in his hoodie pocket!

The Boo didn't seem to like the smell of cabbage pie at all.

"Are you all right?" Mama asked. She didn't look cross any more. She looked worried.

"I'm fine," Dimple snapped.

He hadn't told Mama about the Boo
and he didn't want to. Mama wouldn't
understand why he had it. He didn't
want to share the Boo with anyone.
It was his.

CHAPTER 4
Meanie Mrs Miskin

After dinner, Dimple stomped upstairs to his room.

He made sure the door was shut, then he sat on his bed and took the Boo out of his pocket. It twitched and hummed softly on his hand. Dimple watched.

"**Yucky**," the Boo whispered.

"Listen, Boo," Dimple said. "I don't know what you are, or what to do with you, but please don't shout 'Ewwwww! Yucky!' out loud at dinner even if it *is* cabbage pie."

Blink! Blink! The Boo didn't answer. It just looked at Dimple.

Dimple heard someone whistling. He stood up and put the Boo on the window sill. Then he leaned out to see who was there.

Down below, in the garden next door, an old gnome lady with grey hair and a flowery dress was whistling as she cut roses and put them into a basket.

"That's mean Mrs Miskin," Dimple muttered. "She never gives me back my hoop-balls. Look! There are nine balls down there in her garden! And I've only got one left to play with.

"I never throw them into her garden on purpose and I always ask if she could please throw them back, but she never does.

"I tried knocking on her door to ask if I could get them myself, but she didn't even answer the door. She's *so mean*."

The Boo's frizz stood on end. Then the Boo squirmed and fizzed and made a toy whizzy-kart on the window sill fall onto the floor.

It was at just that moment Mrs Miskin looked up at the window and right at Dimple, who was glaring down at her.

She smiled and waved.

Even though Dimple didn't feel like waving back at mean Mrs Miskin, he decided he should – to be polite. But before he'd even lifted up his hand, the Boo went:

"RASSSSSSSSSSSSP!"

It was SO LOUD. The loudest and rudest raspberry Dimple had ever heard!

He didn't wait to see the look on Mrs Miskin's face. He slammed the window shut and pulled the curtain across it as fast as he could.

CHAPTER 5
The dreadful ding-dong

DING-DONG!

The sun had just gone down when the doorbell rang.

Dimple heard Mama's footsteps clip-clopping along the hall to the front door. He held the Boo tight in his hand and listened hard.

He heard Mama say, "Hello, Mrs Miskin! What a surprise!"

"Uh-oh!" Dimple whispered.

"Meanie Mrs Miskin," the Boo said softly.

Dimple heard the front door click shut, then he heard Mama's shoes clomp up the stairs towards his room. He gulped and quickly put the Boo back into his hoodie pocket.

"Dimple!" Mama's voice sounded cross as she opened the door. "Did you blow a raspberry at Mrs Miskin?"

Dimple didn't say anything. He hoped the Boo would be quiet too.

"Well?" Mama wanted to know. She put her hands on her hips.

"It wasn't me," Dimple began, "it was—"

"Don't fib, young gnome!" Mama sounded very cross now. "You must have blown a VERY loud raspberry because Mrs Miskin is VERY old and she can't hear well. She also told me you slammed your window shut when she waved at you!"

"I did shut the window, but it wasn't me who blew the raspberry ..." Dimple tried again to explain it had been the Boo, but Mama just wasn't listening.

She didn't understand the Boo, or how much Dimple missed PopPop, or how much he hated cabbage pie, or how unfair it was that Mrs Miskin wouldn't give him his hoop-balls back.

"You were rude to me at dinner and now you've been rude to Mrs Miskin," Mama went on. "So it's straight to bed. Now!"

Mama switched off the light.

"Goodnight, Dimple," she said without kissing him. Then she closed the door and left Dimple and the Boo together in the dark.

CHAPTER 6

The feathers

Dimple opened his eyes and yawned. Then he gave his ears a good scratch to wake himself up.

The clock on his toadstool table told him it was almost eight o'clock – time to get up.

Dimple rolled over and …

"WAH!!"

... jumped when he came face to face with the Boo.

Blink! Blink!

In the dim morning light, Dimple thought the Boo looked a bit bigger than before.

But that wasn't the weird thing.

The weird thing was that the Boo was sitting on top of a huge pile of white feathers.

A pile of feathers where Dimple's pillow had been.

"What have you done, Boo?" Dimple asked. "Mama will be very, very angry if she sees! I'll have to hide all the feathers or she won't let me go to the Dragonfly Derby."

Dimple and his friends had been talking about the Dragonfly Derby for weeks. They were going on a school trip to see it.

Dimple picked up handfuls of white feathers and stuffed them into drawers and behind the books on the shelf while he told the Boo all about it.

"It'll be SO exciting!" Dimple squealed. "Sixteen giant dragonflies have to race around Lily Lagoon ten times.

"Mama told me they fly so fast it's hard to even see them – they're just a blur! I can't wait for this trip. It's just what I need to cheer me up."

When Dimple had hidden the last feather, he pulled on his boots and squished the Boo into his hoodie pocket.

"We'd better get going, Boo. Hiding all those pillow feathers has made me late."

CHAPTER 7

The turn in the weather

"Hurry up, Dimple! You mustn't be late for the Dragonfly Derby trip and I need to get to work."

Mama handed Dimple his packed lunch. He didn't ask what was in it, just in case it was cold cabbage-pie leftovers.

"Thanks, Mama," Dimple called, and rushed off to his whizzy-kart.

Dimple put his lunch beside him and checked the Boo was still in his pocket. Then he pressed the "Go" button on the steering wheel and off he whizzed.

"I'm still missing PopPop," Dimple told the Boo, "but nothing is going to spoil today!"

Dimple loved zooming around in his whizzy-kart.

As he whizzed over Zig-Zag Bridge, a big black cloud dimmed the sun.

As he whizzed through Whistling Wood, a few drops of rain specked the windscreen.

As he whizzed over Bluebell Hill, the raindrops began to fall in fat, heavy blobs.

And as he whizzed through the school gates, there was a deafening *CLAP!* of thunder.

With his lunch tucked under his arm and his hood pulled over his ears, Dimple rushed inside to his classroom, where his friends were all chatting about the trip.

"There you are, Dimple!" said Mr Tick. "Sit down, everyone, and listen."

The teacher waited for the class to hush.

"Little gnomes and elves! I know you've all been looking forward to today's trip, but I'm afraid I have bad news."

Outside, thunder boomed and rain pelted the windows.

"Sadly, the bad weather means the Dragonfly Derby isn't going to happen today …"

"AWWWWWWWWW!" said all the gnomes and elves at once.

"I'm sorry," Mr Tick said, "but rain like this could hurt the dragonflies'

wings. The derby will still go ahead –
but not today."

Dimple's cheeks burned. He felt the
hot Boo wriggle in his pocket.

"But we will still have fun today," Mr Tick went on. "I've thought of something else exciting for us to do. Our head teacher Miss Stout is going to come into class and we're all going to do ... a SPELLING TEST!"

CHAPTER 8

The spelling mistake

The Boo peered out of Dimple's pocket and blinked.

"The spelling test will be fun!" Mr Tick said. "You can show Miss Stout how good you are at spelling the tricky words."

Dimple groaned. Tricky words were not fun.

"They're called tricky words because they try to trick you," Dimple whispered to the Boo. "They have pesky letters that don't make a noise when you say the word – so how do you know where they should be?"

The door creaked open and in walked a short, plump gnome with extra-big ears and glasses.

"Good morning!" Miss Stout said in a high voice. "Shall we begin?"

Mr Tick explained the rules. "I'll read out a tricky word," he said. "Put your hand up if you can spell it. The first word is ... LISTEN."

Next to Dimple, an elf called Mint put her hand up. Mr Tick pointed to her.

"L. I. S. **T**. E. N.," she said with a happy grin.

Miss Stout clapped her hands. "Very good! Next!"

"The next word is AUTUMN," said Mr Tick.

"Me!"

"Me!"

"Me!"

Lots of Dimple's friends knew how to spell "autumn".

Dimple huffed. The Boo growled.

"The next word is LAMB," Mr Tick went on.

"L. A. M. **B**.!" a gnome called Shadow shouted out.

"Very good," said Mr Tick. "Ah! Now here is one lots of you will know: GNOME."

"I know this one! It has a silent 'G'!" Dimple whispered to the Boo, and he stuck his hand up.

"Go ahead, Dimple," said Mr Tick.

"N. **G**. O. M. E.," Dimple spelled out.

Mint giggled. Behind Dimple, some other gnomes and elves began to laugh.

"How can you not know how to spell gnome?" Mint asked. "You ARE a gnome!"

Now everyone was laughing.

In Dimple's hoodie pocket, the Boo was grunting and hissing.

The Boo had had enough.

CHAPTER 9
The Boo hullabaloo

Everyone was laughing at Dimple and suddenly the Boo started to bounce around in his pocket. Dimple's tummy felt like it was going to burst.

His cheeks felt hot. He made his hands into fists. His feet twitched under his desk.

Mr Tick shouted, "That's enough!" but the little gnomes and elves were laughing so hard they didn't hear their teacher.

Suddenly, the Boo bounced out of Dimple's pocket and landed on the desk.

"RAAAAAAAAGGHH!"

the Boo roared. It pounded on the wood, over and over again, until ...

CRACK!

... the top of the desk split in two.

"Dimple!" boomed Miss Stout.

"RASSSSSSSSSSPPPP!"

The Boo blew the most ENORMOUS raspberry at Miss Stout. It made her ears flap.

"I **hate cabbage pie!**" yelled the Boo.

The Boo flung itself at the wall and ripped the drawings pinned there.

"I **want my hoop-balls back!**" yelled the Boo.

The Boo picked up a book and hurled it at the window.

"**No one listens!**"

"I want to go to the Dragonfly Derby!"

"I HATE tricky words and ..."

The Boo kicked the classroom door, over and over again, until Dimple thought his own foot was hurting.

"I DON'T LIKE BEING LAUGHED AT."

The whole class was silent now.

"And I really miss PopPop," Dimple said softly.

"Dimple," said Miss Stout. "Come to my office, please."

CHAPTER 10

The Boo did it

Dimple sat silently in Miss Stout's office. The Boo trembled in his pocket.

"I came as soon as I could!" came a very loud voice.

"Huh?"

Mrs Miskin walked through the door.

Dimple looked at her. What was she doing here?

"Dimple's mama was on her way to work, so she asked me to come," Mrs Miskin told the head teacher.

Miss Stout left the room and Mrs Miskin sat down next to Dimple.

"What happened?" she asked. "Your teacher told me you did some very bad things."

"It wasn't me!" Dimple cried. "The Boo did it!"

Mrs Miskin held Dimple's hand. "What's the Boo?" she asked. "Can you show me?"

"It's in here," Dimple said, pointing at his tummy, "but I don't want to show you."

"Then tell me about the Boo instead."

Dimple told Mrs Miskin about how he found the Boo after PopPop left, and how the Boo had shouted "Yucky!" at the cabbage pie, and how the Boo had blown a raspberry at her.

"Oh, yes," said Mrs Miskin. "That was rather rude!"

"You never give my hoop-balls back!"
Dimple said.

"Hoop-balls?" Mrs Miskin asked.

"Yes! There are nine of my hoop-balls
in your garden under the rose bushes! I
tried to ask you for them, over the fence.
I even rang your doorbell to see if I could
get them myself, but you didn't answer!"

"Oh dear!" Mrs Miskin laughed. "My ears are big, but they don't hear very well. When the post gnome comes, he has to blow a trumpet through my letterbox to get me to answer the door! I must need new glasses too. I didn't see your hoop-balls, Dimple."

Now Dimple understood.

"I'm sorry," he whispered.

"Why did the Boo do all those bad things?" Mrs Miskin asked.

"I think it's because it was ... cross," Dimple said softly.

"Is it the Boo who gets cross, Dimple?" asked Mrs Miskin. "Or is it really you? Why don't you talk to someone when you're cross and upset instead of pinning the blame on the Boo?"

"Who can I talk to?" Dimple asked.

"Me," said Mama. She was standing in the doorway.

CHAPTER 11

The lompit

Back at home, Dimple was surprised to see a pile of feathers and his ripped-up pillow on the kitchen table.

He thought Mama might shout at him, but instead she stroked his cheek, then gave him a hug.

"I found them after you left for school,"
she said. "What you did was wrong, but
I think you have been feeling upset and
angry. You should have told me."

"I didn't know how," Dimple muttered.

Mama pointed at the feathers. "When
you need to talk to me but you don't know
how," she said, "you can give me one of
these feathers and I'll help you."

Dimple picked one up. It felt soft and cool in his fingers. He handed it to Mama and then he told her about everything he'd been feeling. He told her about the Boo too.

When they had finished talking, Dimple felt much better.

"Keep your feathers safe." Mama smiled.

Dimple grabbed a handful and stuffed them in his pocket. But when he pulled out his hand, he was holding something else.

The thing was bright red, round – and shiny.

It was just a lompit.

*

Two weeks later, PopPop came home. Dimple hugged him very, very hard.

"I have good news!" PopPop told Dimple and Mama. "A new whizzy-kart factory is opening not far from here. I won't have to go away any more!"

"Yay!" Dimple cheered. "I have good news too! The Dragonfly Derby is tomorrow – we can all go together! Can we play outside now?"

Out in the yard, Dimple looked on the ground for his hoop-balls.

"Bother!" he murmured. "I've only got three. Don't worry, PopPop, I know what to do!"

Dimple reached behind the lompit tree and pulled out his old toy trumpet.

PARP! PARP! PARP!

He tooted it loudly. A few moments later ...

BOING! BOING! BOING!

One by one, all Dimple's hoop-balls
bounced over the fence.

"There you are, Dimple!" shouted Mrs
Miskin. "Have fun!"

Our books are tested
for children and young people by
children and young people.

Thanks to everyone who consulted on
a manuscript for their time and effort in
helping us to make our books better
for our readers.

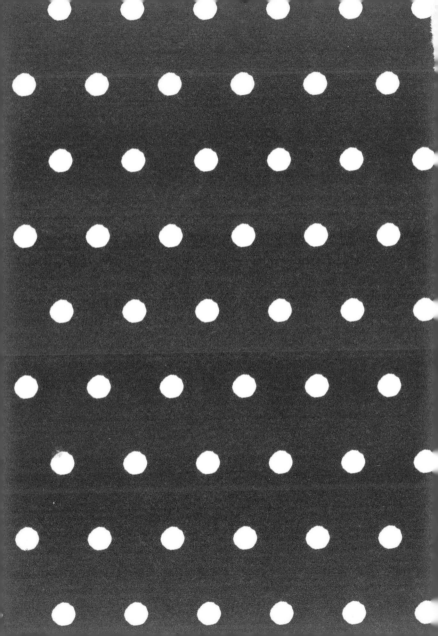